THE

BEACH

WRITTEN BY HELEN DEPREE
ILLUSTRATED BY LINDA McCLELLAND

Waves whisper.
Waves roar.

I whisper.
I roar.

Sea gulls hover.
Sea gulls soar.

4

I hover.
I soar.

Crabs scuttle.
Crabs hide.

I scuttle.
I hide.

Seals dive.
Seals glide.

I dive.
I glide.
I love the beach!

8